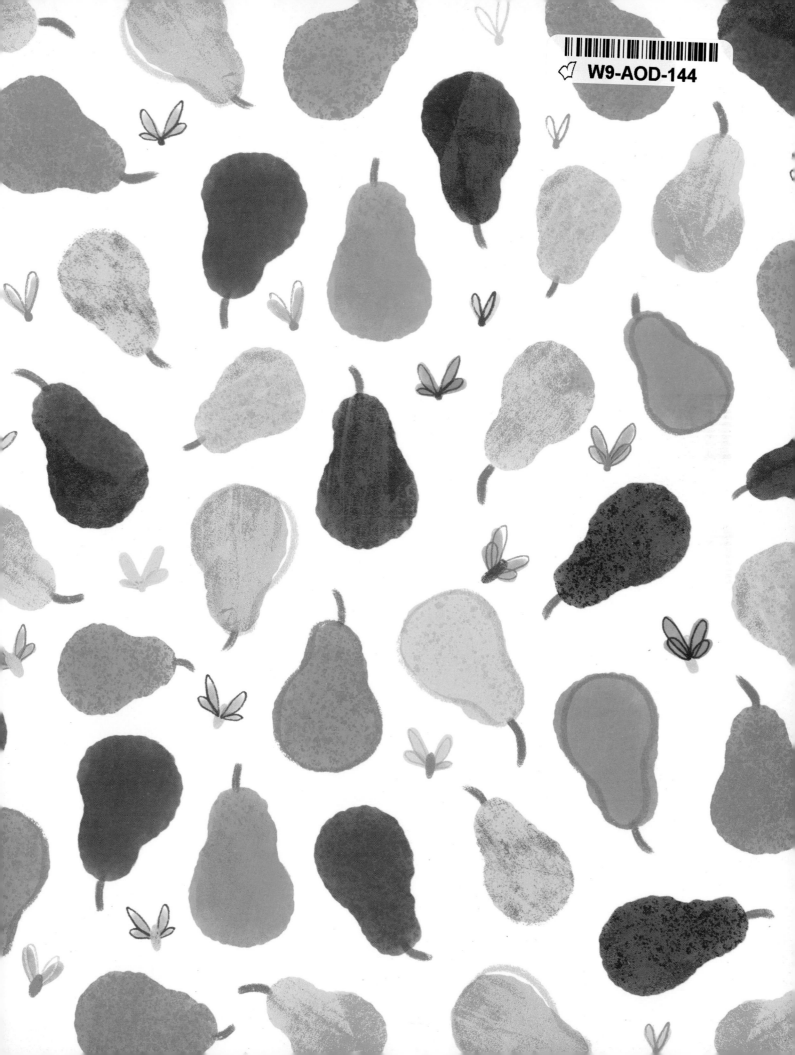

FAIR SHARES

Pippa Goodhart   Anna Doherty

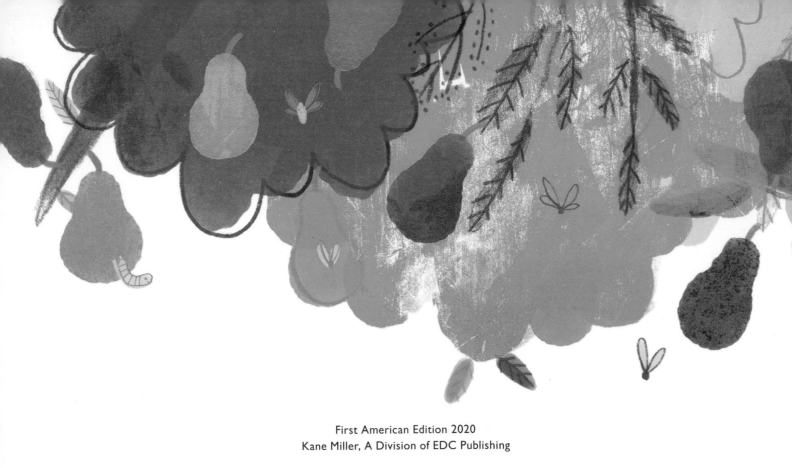

First American Edition 2020
Kane Miller, A Division of EDC Publishing

First published in the UK in 2019 by Tiny Owl Publishing, London
Text copyright © 2019 by Pippa Goodhart
Illustrations copyright © 2019 by Anna Doherty
The moral rights of the author and illustrator have been asserted.

For information contact:
Kane Miller, A Division of EDC Publishing
P.O. Box 470663,
Tulsa, OK 74147-0663
www.kanemiller.com
www.usbornebooksandmore.com

Library of Congress Control Number: 2019952395

Printed in China
ISBN: 978-1-68464-048-5
1 2 3 4 5 6 7 8 9 10

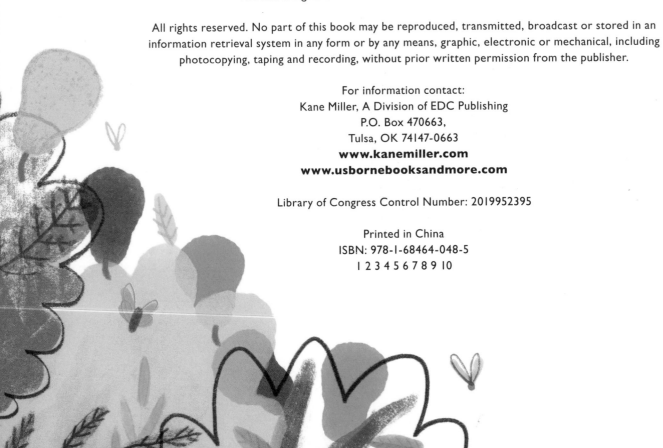

FAIR
SHARES

PIPPA GOODHART

ANNA DoHErty

Kane Miller
A DIVISION OF EDC PUBLISHING

"Oooh, a pear tree full of fruit!" said Hare.

"I'd like to eat one of those pears."

BOING!

BOING!

Hare leapt up, but...

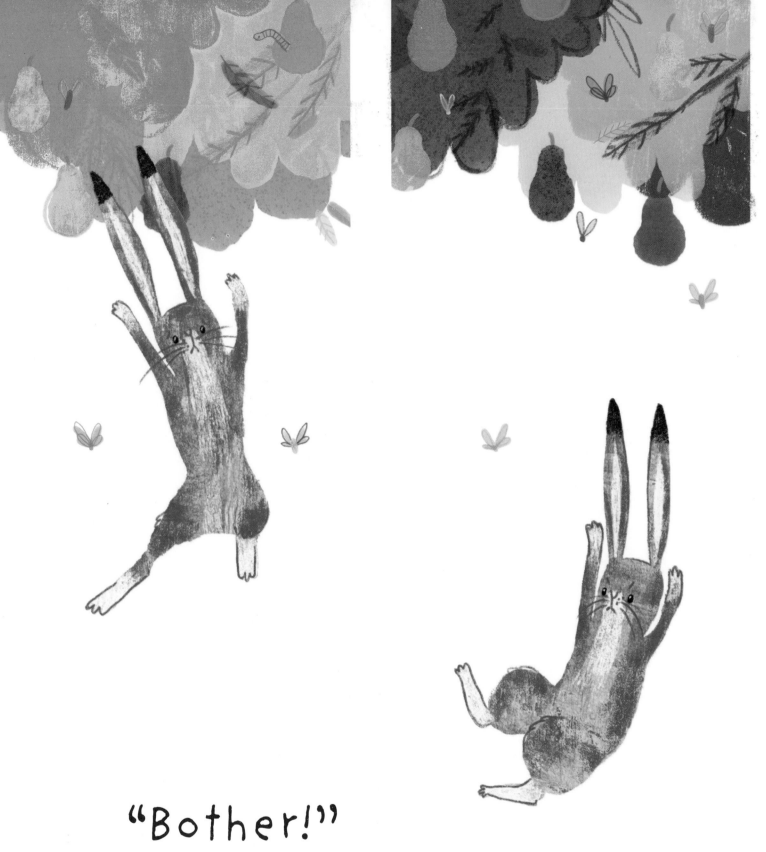

"Bother!"

said Hare.

"Aha," said Bear. "I see lots of pears for me! I'll be able to reach them easily."

But actually...

...she couldn't reach the pears either.

"Bother,"
said Bear.

"Bear," said Hare.
"I know how to
reach the pears."

"How?"
said Bear.

"Well, we haven't
got any steps or stairs,
but we could stand
on chairs!"

"Brilliant!"
said Bear.

"I'll share them out," said Hare.
"One chair for me.
One chair for you, Bear.
Another chair for me.
The end!"

"Oi!" said Bear.

"You've got twice as many chairs as I have!" said Bear.

"That's not fair!"

"Oh, sorry," said Hare. "OK, we can have one chair each, and I'll leave the spare chair over there."

"Yes, that'll be fair,"
said Bear.

"But I **STILL** can't reach a pear!
This doesn't **FEEL** fair at all!" said Hare.

PICK went Bear. **SCRUNCH-MUNCH.**

"*Delicious,*" said Bear.

"Er, excuse me,"
said a tiny voice.

"Who said that?"
said Bear.

"Me,"
said Beetle,
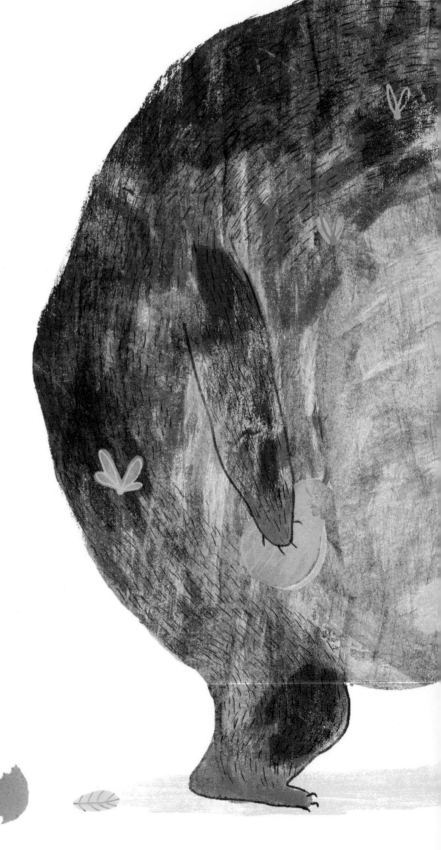
down below.

"I just thought
you should know
that giving
everybody the
same thing isn't
always fair."

"Isn't it?"
said Bear.

"No," said Beetle.
"Let me show you...

"Hare needs two
chairs to reach
the pears...

...but you, Bear,
only need one."

"That's true!" said Hare. "So it is fair for Bear to have one chair, and for me to have two. Wahoo!"

So everyone was happy, until...

"Uh-oh!" said Bear.

"This **STILL** isn't fair. You haven't got **ANY** chairs or pears, Beetle. Would you like a pear?"

"No, thank you," said Beetle. "I don't like pears."

"Oh," said Hare. "What do you like to eat, then?"

Meet the creators

Author

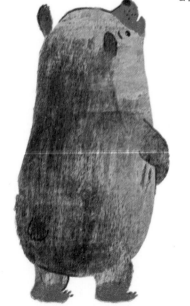

Pippa Goodhart

We all get cross when something isn't fair. "That's not fair!" we say. But making things fair isn't always as simple as just giving everybody the same. We are all different, with different likes and needs. I find that interesting and important, so that's why I wrote a story about it.

I really enjoyed working with Pippa's words and characters to bring the story to life with pictures. It was lovely to explore what the characters looked like, what color they might be and what expressions they had. I mostly work digitally, so I used lots of different Photoshop tools, but I also scanned textures I made with ink and pencil into the computer to make the animals' fur, the plants and the bugs.

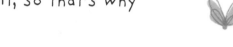 Illustrator

Anna Doherty